THROUGH THE STORMS

A SEVEN WARDENS STORY

SKYE MACKINNON

LAURA GREENWOOD

Peryton Press

CONTENTS

Please note that the authors of this book are from the UK, and as such, spellings and some turns of phrase will appear in British English.

BLURB

Bullied and lonely, young beithir Amber is not having the best of times at Ben Vair, a college for supernatural teenagers.

Until Izban arrives, a mage who is much more than he seems... and his blue hair is rather sexy, too. But when she agrees to help him on his quest, she gets more than she bargained for.

Which may not be such a bad thing.

THE ORIGINAL MYTH

Described as the largest and most deadly kind of serpent, beithirs live in mountain caves and valleys. When stung by a beithir, the victim much reach the nearest body of water to be cured, before the beithir gets there itself (in which case they would die). Beithir is Scottish Gaelic for a variety of words, including "serpent", "lightning" and "thunderbolt".

*To anyone who was bullied at school. And to the
dangerous beasts they've probably become.*

GLOSSARY

Aos Sìth - Fairy Folk

Baoban Sìth - incubus (pronounced Bah-van Shee)

Beithir - Venomous Reptile, a cross between a snake and a dragon

Creideamh Sìth - also known as 'fairy faith', a set of beliefs for living in harmony with the Aos Sìth

Epona - Goddess of Horses

Sgain-dubh - single-bladed knife worn as a part of traditional Scottish Highland dress

1

They'd stolen her tail! Again. It should have been getting old, but Amber was just as angry as she had been the first time. Stealing a beithir's tail should be a crime. Well, it probably was, but nobody cared to punish those girls. They did whatever they wanted, and if that included bullying one of their fellow students, so be it.

At this school, the teachers swore by the motto to let the pupils fight it out amongst themselves. It was supposed to make them stronger. Well, without her tail, Amber was nothing. She was going to have to grow a new one.

She sighed. Would this drama never end? Yes, it would. Only eight months to go until she'd graduate from Ben Vair College. It couldn't come soon enough.

If only Mrs Battleboard hadn't told the class that story about beithirs. Before, everyone assumed she was a snake shifter, a harmless one at that. They may have seen she had a tail even in her human form, but she usually kept it well hidden under baggy shirts. Luckily, they didn't have P.E. lessons at college; she would have dreaded changing in front of the other girls. It was normal for her to see her tail sitting just above her bum, but not for the others.

So she'd ignored them, they'd ignored her and she'd been fine with that. Now, they knew differently. They knew she was a relic who could regrow her own tail, just like lizards. And they saw it as a challenge to find out how often she could do it.

She'd grown to hate their transformation classes every Thursday. She'd never seen the point in them either. She'd been born being able to shift, not like some of the others who'd had to learn it. It was second nature to her, no, it *was* her nature. Nowadays, she spent the entire lesson trying to hide from Tamsin and her friends. They were a wolf pack who had become excellent snake hunters. She'd lost count of how often they'd cornered her and ripped off her tail. If she got it back within a few minutes, she could reattach it, but of course they never let her do that.

If only she had her beithir powers already, but they usually manifested in la beithir's early twenties, and she'd only just turned eighteen. If she had them... they'd never hurt her again. But for now, she could just as well be a snake shifter - without a tail.

She bumped into something hard and was ripped from her self-pitying thoughts. Something... no, someone blue was looking down at her, obviously displeased she'd not looked where she was going.

It was a man, his hair blue like cornflowers, his ears pierced with dozens of silver rings. He looked so out of place here that she had a hard time not to stare. Ben Vair was a boring, down-to-earth place, if you ignored the fact that all of the students had some kind of supernatural power. There were no punks here. And yet...

"Do I have something on my face?" he asked in annoyance, rubbing his chest where she'd rammed against him.

"No, sorry," she mumbled and turned to leave, hoping he'd forget her. She was in enough trouble already, and not having her tail was making her even less self-confident around others. It also disturbed her sense of balance. It would take at least two days for it to grow back, and even longer to be back to its old length. And for that, she'd need to go down to the secret lab beneath the school to recharge. At least no one else knew about it, and she'd have some peace for a change.

"Bugger off," the man growled and she fled, ignoring the giggles of the other students as she ran through the corridors to her dorm. It was the only good thing about staying at Ben Vair: having a room of her own. Originally, the dorm was meant for six girls, but there weren't enough sixth form students in her year to fill it. The others preferred to squeeze into one room rather than share with her. Amber didn't have a problem with that. She liked her solitude. It gave her space to think.

Right now, she was thinking about the strange blue-haired man she'd bumped into. He looked too old to be a student. But Ben Vair would never employ someone like him as a teacher. The professors here were old and traditional. Even the younger ones behaved as if they were ancient. It seemed to be in the job description that to work here, they needed to be boring. She had no idea where all the good teachers went after their training. There weren't that many supernatural schools out there. She knew of one other in Scotland, and a few more down in England and Wales.

She sat down on her bed, wincing at the reminder that her tail wasn't where it was supposed to be. Such a strange feeling. Did the others ever feel the absence of their tails? Or were they used to it, having been born without one?

For a beithir, a tail was a sign of pride. Amber's mother had hers adorned with rings and colourful tattoos. She herself had had two little rings on hers... before the whole drama started. Now she didn't bother with it. Maybe once she'd left school she could go back to making herself look pretty. Until then, she was going to have to keep her head down and pretend to be invisible.

Which involved not bumping into strangers.

She groaned. She'd made a fool of herself. Again. If she hadn't been one of the college's best students, she'd probably have been expelled a long time ago. Chaos and misfortune followed her, no matter what she did. Maybe it was her beithir heritage. Maybe some of the legends describing her kind as the bringers of doom were true. But her family had made sure to disprove that rumour. Her parents were respected, much-loved pillars of their community, and with Amber's older sister working in the local nursing home, they were all assets rather than a nuisance to their surroundings. But not her.

She lay down and stared at the bare ceiling. When she first moved into the dorm, she'd drawn little stars on it with a white pen. They were almost invisible unless you knew what you were looking for. It was one of her many secrets.

SHE WALKED into class with her head down, hoping no one would notice she'd arrived. It was a stupid thing to try, really. There were only ten others in the class, one person entering the room was going to be noticed.

"I see you've finally joined us," an unfamiliar voice said. Amber looked up, surprised to find the blue haired man she'd run into the other day sat at the teacher's desk.

"Sorry, sir," she muttered, making her way towards her desk. He'd better get used to her being a few minutes late every lesson. It was her way of at least trying to avoid Tamsin.

She sat down, pulling out her notepad and pens. Now that she was here, she'd be the best student blue-hair had ever had. Not that he looked old enough to have had many. He couldn't be much older than her. Twenty-four maybe?

"Where's Professor Shales?" Becky asked. A good question from one of Tamsin's lackeys there. She guessed miracles did happen on occasion.

"She's sick," blue-hair answered. Amber raised her eyebrows, but didn't say anything. It seemed unlikely that the bear shifter was ill. They were notoriously sturdy creatures.

The class tittered. Apparently, she wasn't the only one to make that observation. It made sense others would. For all their faults, only the smartest stayed on to study at Ben Vair.

"Alright, calm down," blue-hair commanded. Hmm. His demeanour had changed completely. Whereas before he'd seemed laid back but unapproachable, now he was actually commanding the attention of the room. It was a little disconcerting, but that pretty much summed up school in general.

"I'm not sure exactly where you're up to, but I've been led to understand you're about to start studying storm magic. I want you to get into pairs and try the exercise on page three hundred and ninety-four of your textbooks."

The sound of eleven people opening their books all at once filled the room.

"But, sir?" Tamsin asked, only raising her hand after starting to speak. "We can't do that exercise in the classroom." As per usual, Amber noticed Tamsin had only glanced at her book once, and certainly not for long enough to read the large letters saying: *to be done outside.*

Blue-hair scowled at her. Amber wasn't sure why he hadn't told them his name yet. Most of the teachers seemed to enjoy the power trip it brought.

"If you'd read the instructions properly, Miss Garou, you'd know we need to go outside for this particular exercise."

Amber hated to admit it, but she liked the way he spoke, or maybe she just liked the way he was putting Tamsin in her place.

"But-"

"Get yourself into pairs, and follow me outside." Blue-hair busied himself with his things, and Amber watched as her classmates paired up. It was the same five pairs as always, then her. Why hadn't the school offered a place to a twelfth student? Almost all their practical lessons involved splitting into pairs. Which meant Amber was on her own at least twice a day.

The class trailed after blue-hair, all chuntering

about going outside in the rain. All except Amber. Even if she had someone to chunter to, she wouldn't. She loved the rain. It was where she felt strongest. It wouldn't regrow her tail though. More's the pity.

Her classmates squared off against one another and began to try and cast a storm. She hung back. Not only was she partnerless, but without her beithir powers, there was no chance she'd be able to summon any kind of storm. Therefore, it seemed better to hang back and disappear into the background.

"Miss Beithir, you should be practicing." Blue-hair appeared next to her, a stern look on his face.

"I don't have a partner," she mumbled. There was something about him that had her on the back foot, and she didn't like it at all.

Blue-hair sighed. "Right, yes an unlucky class of eleven."

"I'd hardly call the others unlucky," she responded.

"But you would yourself? I think you may be letting what you are define you too much, Miss Beithir."

"Bit hard not to," she muttered. Especially when her very name was a reminder. "I prefer to be called Amber." She lifted her chin defiantly.

"You can work with me then, Amber." His lips quirked into a smile.

"Thanks." She tried to be sincere, she really did. But she'd much rather just slip by unnoticed.

He rolled up his sleeves, revealing colourful tattoos stretching all the way across his skin. Or all the way that Amber could see. Thoughts of how far they went passed through Amber's mind, but she quickly dismissed them. *These* weren't the kind of thoughts she should be having about a teacher, even a substitute one.

"Do I get to know my partner's name?" she asked, surprising herself. She wasn't normally so confident, especially around people she hadn't met before. Or teachers. She especially didn't trust teachers.

"Izban - err - Mr Smith." He coughed as he corrected himself.

Amber frowned. Why would a teacher accidentally introduce himself as the wrong name? Obviously she was right about him being new to the job, otherwise he'd never have made such an obvious slip up.

"Well, Izban - err - Mr Smith, I hope you're ready to watch the most pathetic storm conjuring ever."

He ignored her attempt at making fun of his

name. "Let's start with looking at the instructions together," he said. "Where's your book?"

Amber was kicking herself inside. So much for going under the radar. "I left it inside."

A frown was appearing on his forehead so she quickly added, "I don't need it. I've got a photographic memory."

"Oh yes, I've heard that about beithirs." He was suddenly looking very curious. "Do all of your kind have that?"

She shrugged. "As far as I know. It's not something special for us. I didn't know not everybody could recall things like I do until I came to Ben Vair." Now that she'd lived among both humans and supernaturals for a while, she was convinced that the conception of snakes being intelligent was based on beithirs.

"Fascinating," he murmured, looking at her as if she was a specimen waiting to be studied. She wasn't sure if she liked being looked at like that. "Let's begin - without your book."

He smiled at her, making him seem like a very different person. But as soon as he stepped away to give her space for the conjuring, he turned into the stern teacher again. Curious.

She looked around. The five pairs were in

various stages of success and failure. With a satisfying smirk, she noticed that Tamsin was having trouble controlling the tiny bolts of lightning flashing above her head. Her dark hair was beginning to stand up, destroying her carefully pruned hairdo. Meghan, one of the nicer girls in her class, was swaying her hands above her head, seemingly in total sync with the storm clouds she had conjured. Now if only Amber could do the same...

She sighed and began with the first step in the instructions. Visualise a storm. She huffed. Now that could be anything. A little rainstorm? A summer thunderstorm? A hurricane?

"What's wrong?" her teacher asked and she sighed again. Could this lesson please be over?

"What kind of storm are we supposed to conjure?" she asked and watched in surprise as his eyes lit up.

"Excellent question. Strange that nobody else has asked that. They've all jumped straight into the exercise." He seemed genuinely puzzled by that. What a weird man. "Let's start with something small. A cloud and some lightning, perhaps?"

Amber nodded even though she knew she wouldn't achieve either. She didn't have much magic, and the powers she had were not related to storm conjuring. Not at all. But at this school, everybody needed to go to all the lessons, no matter how irrelevant. Others got additional tutoring in the afternoons, depending on their abilities and species, but so far, nobody had bothered to give her those extra lessons. She was quite glad about that. She excelled in theoretical subjects, partly thanks to her memory, but the practical studies... yuck. They usually ended in her being tailless.

Oh well, she wasn't going to achieve anything by standing here, lost in self-pity. She squared her shoulders and pictured a cloud. Grey, dark, foreboding. About half as tall as she was and just as wide. She added some shading and swirls for good measure. It was just like painting a picture. Except that she was great at art, but not so good with magic. When she had a perfect cloud, she breathed it out of her mind, just like it said in her textbook. She wasn't sure how that was even supposed to work. But that's what it said, 'Breathe out the magic.' Had the people writing it been on some kind of psychedelic drug? She wouldn't be surprised.

She opened her eyes to look at her work. Nothing. Not even a tiny speck of a cloud. Deflated, she sighed. She'd known it from the beginning. She was useless at this. Why did the teachers keep forcing her to try? There was no point.

She was never going to be a mage. Not like him. She could smell it. Opening her mouth ever so slightly, she tasted the air around her. Yup, definitely mage. She may not have a forked tongue in her human form, but she still had the senses of a snake.

"Try again," he said, ignoring the blush on her cheeks. Failure. She was such a damn failure.

"It won't work," she replied, staring down at the ground. "I don't have magic to do that kind of thing. I can shift, that's about it."

"Everybody has magic inside of them, even humans. But not everybody knows how to access it. That's why you're here, to learn how to do it. How to fulfil your potential. And once you find your magic, you'll find your destiny."

She looked up at him, open-mouthed. "Did you seriously just say 'destiny'? That's a bit over the top."

He stayed serious. "Apparently, I need to have a chat with the Headmistress. It's appalling that you're not taught your true value and purpose. How are you supposed to be motivated if they don't teach you what your strengths are?"

Ignoring her, he turned around and left, muttering under his breath. She stared at him in confusion. What just happened? Did he really just leave the class on their own?

She looked around. To her great pleasure, Tamsin's eyebrows had a new, singed and smoky look. It suited her... not. Another girl, Anna, was fighting an enormous windhose. A teacher would have come in handy here to help her. But Mr Smith had left. What a weirdo.

Amber looked at her watch and shrugged. It was almost the end of the lesson anyway. With nobody here to stop her, she could just as well leave and do something worthwhile. Like painting.

She headed to the college's studio on the top floor. It was a former attic that the arts teacher, Mrs Mumbly, had refurbished into a bright, welcoming room. This was Amber's second refuge. Any time she didn't spend in her dorms, she spent here among the canvases and the smell of paint.

There was nobody around; she had the studio for herself. Good. She picked up one of the easels and moved it to a skylight at the end of the room. If she stretched, she could just about see out of the window. In the far distance were the rolling hills of the Lowlands, some of them covered in clouds. Between the hills and the school were several rivers and a lot of farmland, but she couldn't see that from here. So she focused on the mountains instead.

She chose a large, square canvas and then went over to the shelf where Mrs Mumbly stored the paints. Everybody painted hills in green, so she was not going to choose that colour. A bottle of azure blue called to her. Why not. Nobody was going to see the painting anyway. It was something she did for herself, not for others. Her teacher was probably the only one who ever saw her paintings, and that simply because she had to leave them here to dry until she could take them to her room.

Taking a large brush, she covered the canvas in blue paint. A solid foundation, her old arts teacher at primary school used to say. Of course, back then she'd only drawn stick figures and misshapen animals. Now, she was trying to depict real life, but usually, she failed at it. Her paintings turned out abstract even when she didn't intend them to. Still, she enjoyed the peaceful feel of the brush touching the canvas, even though she wasn't always happy with the result.

That blue... it reminded her of something. Discarding the brush, she dipped a finger into the paint and drew a rough shape on the canvas. Her motions were fluid, almost automatic. She let her mind drift and her artistic sense took over.

An hour later, Amber was staring at her painting. And wasn't sure what to think. It was weird. That was the only word to describe it, really. It was the silhouette of a man, with a large symbol in the foreground. It looked Celtic, with lots of knots and pretty swirls. Thing was, Amber didn't know anything about Celtic symbols. So why had she drawn one?

It had to be just a random shape, a pattern that her mind came up with. And the man... surely it only looked like Mr Smith because of the blue colour. The same colour as his hair. Yup, total coincidence.

For once, she didn't leave the canvas in the studio. She carefully carried it back to her room, making sure the paint didn't run. There, she put it on her window sill, continuing to look at it. It had to be the strangest painting she'd ever done. She rarely painted people, they were hard to make recognisable and she didn't like it when they turned out looking like someone else. But with him... it was definitely Mr Smith. No doubt about it.

Was she turning into one of those teenage girls who had a crush on their teachers? She surely hoped not. She was too old for that, and he wasn't even *that* good looking. Interesting, mysterious, yes, but hot... no. She wasn't really into piercings either.

The dinner bell rang and her rumbling stomach told her how hungry she was. Since lunchtime she'd lost her tail, bumped into a blue-haired man who turned out to be her teacher, failed at conjuring a storm and painted the very same man. What a day.

2

hy was the library at this damn school so big? It made it ten times more difficult for Izban to find what he needed. When his grandfather had sent him here to find a specific book, he'd figured it'd be a quick in and out job. That'd all gone wrong when the Headmistress had caught him sneaking in. He'd had to say he was a supply teacher just to get out of that one.

Though from what he'd seen today, he'd do a damn sight better job if he was actually a teacher here. How they weren't teaching their students their true potential was beyond him. Everyone had magic, it was just a case of showing them how to tap into it. And the beithir girl...she had buckets of it. He could sense it rolling off her, even if she didn't seem to think she had it. He wondered what was up with that, but he couldn't waste time thinking on it. There was far too much at stake to get distracted by a pretty redhead.

Dust had settled on the shelves in front of him, so thickly that he almost couldn't tell where one book started and another ended. Whatever was happening at this school, care-taking and teaching weren't it. He trailed his finger across the spines, feeling the old cracked leather beneath the dust. Drawing his hand away wasn't pleasant though. Not with all the dirt now caked on his finger. He couldn't even wipe it off without leaving a stain.

He sighed. He had to look through the books one way or another, otherwise he'd never find the book Epona was supposed to have written. He had doubts over his grandfather's sanity on this one. For a start, he highly doubted a goddess would write a book at all. There wasn't even any evidence that the gods existed after all. But also, even if she had, what use was anything the goddess of horses had written? He was a mage. He hadn't even been near a horse in...forever really.

But, what his grandfather wanted, his grandfather got. So long as he didn't manage to link it all back to the Seven Wardens prophecy, it was fine by Izban. That one he really was fed up of. He'd been told it so many times during his childhood, and there was always a knowing look in his grandfather's eye while he recounted it. Almost like he expected it to come to pass at some point during Izban's lifetime.

Prophecies and the like were all a bunch of codswallop as far as Izban was concerned. None of his people believed in crystal balls, actually no one believed in crystal balls, even the true Romani he'd studied with while living on the continent. He'd laughed when they'd out right admitted that it was all for show. But they did have a point, most humans would believe anything if it gave them a purpose. Most non-humans too if their opinions on prophecy and foretelling were anything to go by.

Elders should always be respected though. And as his grandfather was the Elder Mage, Izban had to do what he was told.

He glanced around, pleased to see he was alone in this section of the library. That meant he could speed the process up at least. He held up his hand, and twisted the simple hawthorn ring he was wearing until a small *aos sìth* appeared in the palm of his hand. He'd never quite worked out whether the creature was male or female, all he knew was it had taken him a long time to get it to actually help him and not just cause chaos. Their peoples had been tied together for centuries through the practice of *creideamh sìth*, and the *aos sìth* was his main source of magic. He just hoped it would never turn on him. He gave his helper enough milk and baked goods to keep it happy though, as tradition dictated.

"Lorg an leabhar mu dhèidhinn Epona!" he whispered. While he was pretty sure his earlier assessment of being alone was correct, he didn't want to risk it. If anyone caught him using magic, there'd be questions. Even if he was in a supernatural school, there was a surprising lack of magic doing about. He guessed that was because a lot of the students were shifters, but even they had the spark inside them. Some even had the potential to be powerful, like the beithir girl.

The *aos sìth* leapt from his hand and flew up and down the books on the shelf, making an odd chittering noise as it did. To anyone who hadn't encountered the creatures before, he was sure it'd be unnerving. But to Izban, the sound actually verged on soothing. He'd grown up around them, and was more than used to it as a result.

It stopped in front of a faded green cover,

discoloured from age and the hundreds of hands that had no doubt touched the leather. Before books like these had become treasures, no one had really cared how they were handled.

"Thanks," he said aloud, despite knowing the *aos sith* already knew that. Their connection was part of the magic of their peoples after all. It chittered again in response, before disappearing into thin air. Which was to be expected. It had done what he'd asked it to, now it would go back to its own plane and gorge itself on milk and bread and the like. He really didn't understand the appeal, but whatever made his little companion happy.

He grimaced as he touched the dust covered book, but carried on anyway, pulling it away from its position on the shelves. The leather was as dry to touch as it looked, and he was already concerned about it not making the journey back to his grandfather. He'd have to bind it in protection spells, which he luckily didn't need the *aos sith* for. They were just for certain types of magic.

He took it over to a small wooden table, and placed it down gently, before sinking into the armchair by the side. At least the school knew how to furnish, even if it didn't know how to do much else.

Carefully, he opened the book, only to have a small mushroom cloud of dust explode in his face. He coughed, and wafted his hand in front of him in an attempt to disperse the damn stuff. If he wasn't so in need of keeping his cover, he'd be in the Headmistress' office right this second giving her a what for about the state of her establishment. He'd almost done that earlier too, after he'd stormed off during his lesson on storms, until he remembered why he couldn't. His mother had always said that his need to do right by everyone was both one of his greatest strengths, and one of his greatest faults. He tended to agree with her. He could really have blown his grandfather's mission, and all for the sake of one little beithir girl.

Once the dust had settled, he looked back at the open page in front of him and groaned. The writing was tiny, and that weird swirly handwriting that medieval folk had been so enamoured with. On the plus side, it appeared to be in Gaelic and not some truly ancient tongue he hadn't mastered yet.

Not that he actually *had* to read it. His grandfather said he wanted the book itself, not a summary, which meant Izban could get away without doing so. But he was curious now.

He flipped a few more pages, disappointed to

discover that a lot of it just seemed to be anatomical sketches of horses. The main curiosity in that being how far ahead of their time whoever wrote this was. Though he supposed anyone could dissect a horse. All they needed was a dead one and a sharp stone. And maybe some water to wash their hands in.

He was beginning to get bored when he flipped onto a page that piqued his interest. Oddly, this one seemed to be labelled *aquine*. At first, he thought it was a spelling error, but on closer inspection, it definitely wasn't, not if the particularly detailed drawing next to it was anything to go by. He studied the text in more detail. Apparently, who ever had written this book, had counted kelpies as the same as horses. He frowned. There was no mention of their own magic, nor their shifting abilities. In fact, if any *real* kelpie saw this, they'd probably rip it to shreds. After claiming it was all the selkies' doing of course. He wasn't sure where the rivalry between the two kinds had come from, but it was almost infamous among the supernatural community.

While it was kind of fascinating reading, he still didn't quite understand the point. There was nothing his grandfather was going to gain from this, he was sure. Maybe the old man was losing his marbles. He hoped not. Technically, Izban was supposed to be his successor, but that would mean returning home for good and no more travelling to learn other magics. He still hadn't been to Africa to learn from the Shamans yet, nor from the Inuits further north. Taking over as the Elder Mage wasn't in his plan for years to come. If only his brother was a bit older, then he could avoid the job altogether.

If only this book was the only thing he needed to get, then he could have left this strange school. But no, his grandfather was being greedy and wanted more. Izban looked at his list. Four more items to go, and all of them stranger than the next. As if a book supposedly written by the goddess of horses wasn't strange enough.

He sighed as he read through the next line of instructions. A red ruby, infused with baobhan sìth saliva. Seriously? This sounded more and more like things charlatans would sell at the carnival. He really didn't want to touch anything that had been 'infused with saliva', especially if it was that of an incubus. He'd never met one of those fae, but maybe it was good that way. He was as straight as they came, but he'd read how nobody could resist the vibes of an incubus in heat. He quite liked his genitals intact, and incubi weren't known to be gentle.

There were no notes about where this ruby might be found. Probably not in the library. Did the school have a vault? Time to find out.

He put the book into one of his magically enhanced coat pockets, which both decreased its size and secured it from both magical influences and pickpockets. He couldn't be careful enough in a place full of naughty teenagers.

Vaults were usually in the basement, so that's where Izban headed next. A door with an old 'staff only' sign made him smirk. It was locked but he didn't even need his *aos sìth* to open it. He'd been cracking locks with magic since he discovered he had it. His parents had hated it.

With a click, the door opened, leading into a dark corridor. He conjured a light to hover in front of him. He'd never been a fan of the dark. There were no lights on the ceiling that he could see. A very old part of the building then. Before they supplied the building with electricity to make it seem more normal to visitors. Humans didn't take kindly to floating balls of light. After a few metres, the corridor forked into two further hallways. Izban randomly chose the right one. It smelled better. The floor became increasingly uneven and he increased the strength of his light. That's when he spotted some cleverly hidden doors built into the walls. Their doors were the same dark stone as the walls and only a thin black outline gave them away. Curious. He wouldn't have noticed them without the extra light.

He tried pushing the first one but it didn't budge. There was no lock that he could see so that kind of magic was useless. He examined it with his magic awareness, but he couldn't detect anything. It just seemed to be a slab of stone.

Time to summon his *aos sìth*, who was going to be rather grumpy about being disturbed again.

Unless it wasn't a magic door at all. Maybe there was a lever somewhere? Izban looked around again. On his left were three doors but the wall on his right was smooth. No buttons, levers, wheels. Nothing.

He walked a bit further along the corridor. It ended in a wooden door, one with a lock this time. Easy. He opened it and stopped in surprise. It was a laboratory, as old fashioned as they came. He cautiously entered the room. There was a cauldron, lots of weird vessels and tubes, and rows upon rows of shelves on the walls, laden with filled glasses. This was an alchemist's paradise. Pity that Izban had no interest whatsoever in all of this. Whenever he tried to produce a potion, it usually ended up as something poisonous or simply an ill-smelling mess. It was not one of his talents, so he'd given up trying to find enthusiasm for the art of potion making long ago.

What he was interested in was a way to open those strange stone doors. Maybe there was a clue in here somewhere?

He looked around, trying to ignore the little creatures floating in some of the glasses. He almost thought he spotted an *aos sìth* in one of them. Gruesome.

3

mber shivered as the cold air hit her skin. She hated coming down here, but she needed to do it if she had any hopes of her tail regrowing soon. There was something restorative in this room apparently. Or at least, that was what the nurse had told her the first time she'd lost her tail.

That time had been a genuine accident. She'd trapped it in a door frame during one of the early shifting classes, and quickly found herself tail-less.

After that, she'd only lost it when someone had detached it. Apparently, she shouldn't have let them know it would regrow. Their theory now was that if it could regrow itself, then it wouldn't hurt.

The idiots. Of course it hurt. If one of them had their fingernails pulled out it'd still hurt, and they'd grow back. Amber had considered doing it to them in their sleep more than once, but had decided against it. She didn't want to give them the satisfaction of knowing they got to her that much.

A loud creaking noise filled the room, worrying her slightly. The entrance to it was hidden, and she was the only student with a key. As she should be. She was the only student who was also a beithir. The rest of them didn't need a room to regrow body parts. Especially not regularly.

So no one should be around. Not to mention they should all be asleep. It was well past lights out, and none of them wanted to risk the intense scolding that would come from the headmistress. No one knew what kind of supernatural she was, but she tended to spew a little bit of fire whenever she was angry. If a student wanted to keep their clothing intact, then they didn't make her angry. It was as simple as that.

The creaking sound came again, and she turned slightly, trying to see what was happening over by the door. Times like this, she wished she didn't have to stand with her back to it. Or stand there naked.

The magic needed both to work, annoyingly, so she had no choice. Didn't mean she had to be comfortable with that though.

"Hello?" she called out. At least she was still in human form. She rarely turned into a beithir at school. Or not a full one anyway. She'd dwarf the other students if she did. But she could do partial shifts, and often had to.

She heard the scuffing of shoes against the hard floor and a mild panic took hold. Her mind flitted between running for her clothes, and shifting so she could protect herself. Maybe this was the origin of the human concept of fight or flight.

"Hello?" she repeated. This time, there was a small cough in return, one that sounded worryingly male. Shifting it was. Without knowing who it was, she didn't want to be caught in human form at all. There was more than one male student here she tried to avoid one on one time with, thankfully they were in other years. And if it was someone that didn't go to the school...well she certainly didn't want them to see her naked. She may be a shifter, but she still had her insecurities.

Amber reached down deep inside herself, and pulled the shift outwards. She'd never understood how it worked, but it was almost like something unfolded from the centre of her chest outwards. As the shift progressed, scales began to cover her skin, and her long red hair turned into a ridge of webbing down her neck and back. She used to hate the slightly grey tint to her green scales, but once she'd accepted their use, things changed. Now, she loved them, and not just because she'd be able to hide against the storm clouds easily in this form.

A deep longing filled her. She hadn't flown in ages. School had an annoying no flying rule that meant she couldn't. And she wouldn't be able to go home until the summer. It was a frustrating catch-22. By then, there wouldn't be nearly as many storms.

The shift was almost complete, and she felt her face lengthening and eyes widening. It was always an odd sensation feeling her eyes slide from the front of her face to the side, but it enhanced her vision a lot. Maybe this would even help her spot whoever it was that was in the room with her.

Maybe it'd even scare them off.

She could dream.

Amber tried to flick her tail from side to side, mostly because she enjoyed it, but partly so she could balance. Except that all she had there was a small stub of one where it had started to grow back. Her eyes narrowed with hatred.

More scuffling sounds came from near the doorway, and she swung her head around in that direction. The sounds were clearer now, but that was likely just her improved hearing making her more attuned to it all.

She lowered her head to the floor and slithered in the direction. She'd forgotten how freeing it felt to be in this form, and the grace with which it moved. It was as natural as her human body to her, and would be even more so once her magic actually set in. But she had years to wait for that still. Some beithirs got their powers early, but no one in her family ever had, so it seemed unlikely that she would either. It was the kind of thing she dreamed of though. No one would mess with a large snake-like creature who emanated lightening. Maybe she'd even breathe it? But that was a skill not many of their people had. Maybe one in a generation? She wasn't sure. It'd been a while since she'd been forced to memorise the family tree and who'd been last to manifest what power.

A piece of rubble chinked against the floor to the other side of the door, and she swung her head to the side, the long whiskers that sprung from her snout swaying with the movement.

She slithered forwards again, and turned the corner, coming face to face with the last person she'd expected to see here.

Not him. Not again. What was it with this man that he appeared wherever she went to? His blue hair was a stark contrast from the dark laboratory around them, but even without it she would have recognised it. Hopefully he hadn't seen her shift, then he wouldn't know who she was. Maybe he'd think her just another snake... okay, a rather large snake with not much of a tail.

He stared at her and she couldn't bring herself to break eye contact. He seemed to be just as transfixed by her as she was by him. What was he doing down here? Did he know this was the place she'd go to? No, it couldn't be. Nobody knew about it besides some of the teachers.

What was she supposed to do now? Slither away and hide? Wait for him to leave? Stay here all night so he wouldn't see her in her human form? Why did he have to come down here? And what was he doing here anyway?

Pity she couldn't ask him while she was in her

beithir shape. While she could communicate mentally with others of her kind, it didn't work with other species, especially not humans. There were rumours that mindtalk was possible with soul mates even if they were not a beithir themselves, but Amber didn't believe in that. Why would anybody be with someone who wasn't a beithir? That was just weird. They would never understand her customs and need to shift from time to time. Her human skin got itchy if she stayed in it for too long. And her tail felt a lot more natural in this form, too. She was used to having it wrapped around her waist as a human, but it wasn't comfortable and the baggy shirts she wore had often resulted in people asking her whether she was pregnant. No, if Amber ever fell in love, it was going to be with another beithir.

But why was she thinking about that? She was supposed to find a solution to her immediate problem: Izban. The blue-haired man was still staring at her as if he'd seen a ghost. She couldn't blame him though. Her kind were notoriously hard to find if you didn't know where to look. As far as Amber knew, she was the first beithir at this school for at least a generation.

"What are you?" the man whispered and she hissed in frustration. Was he expecting her to reply? Seriously? Couldn't he see that her forked tongue didn't lend itself to speaking like a human?

She shook her head and turned, finally breaking eye contact. If he was going to stay, fine, but he wasn't going to stop her from healing. This room held artefacts far more magical than Amber would ever understand. One of them, or several, were responsible for the powers that were now slowly making her tail regrow.

As long as she stayed In the lab, she'd heal. And if Izban had to stay for that, so be it. As long as he didn't attack her. Or take pictures. She hated that. Whoever came up with the idea of putting a camera into a phone? They were everywhere and she had to be careful that pictures of beithirs didn't reach the internet.

Of course, smartphones were forbidden at Ben Vair, as most kinds of supernaturals there were publicity shy. Humans hated what they didn't understand, which was why most of shifters and mages lived in hiding. But there were always some rule breakers who thought that putting a video on Youtube would be fun.

No, it wasn't.

She hissed in irritation at those thoughts. Teenagers were so annoying. They had no sense of responsibility and scale. Most of them would sacrifice the centuries of secrecy their kind had prevailed only to get a few more clicks and views. Pathetic.

"You don't need to be afraid of me," Izban whispered, nearing Amber. She slithered backwards a little. When he continued to follow her, she bared her fangs, glistening with venom. That made him stop in his tracks.

"Okay, you don't have to bite, I'm backing off, see?"

And indeed, he walked back a step or two. Satisfied, she closed her maw. It was good to see a bit of fear from people occasionally. Far too many underestimated her. Just because she didn't bite the girls who ripped off her tail didn't mean she was completely defenceless. But she had principals. And she valued her freedom. Killing people was not going to be in her future, venomous teeth or not.

She'd never tried how poisonous her bite really was, but her parents had taught her that most grown beithirs were easily able to kill a human with their bite. Or even a supernatural.

"I need to look around for something, would you mind leaving me to it?"

He looked almost desperate. She had to laugh - inside, of course, snakes didn't laugh.

She shook her head in a wide gesture, obvious enough so he couldn't miss it.

He huffed. "I don't have time to do this tomorrow. If you don't leave, will you at least promise not to tell anyone I was here?"

She cocked her head. That was a big kind of promise. Usually, she'd set terms, like being able to tell someone if it was endangering him, her or others. But she couldn't speak, damn it.

Maybe she should partially shift. It would mean she could actually talk, and she wouldn't be left totally naked. Kind of. She could leave it so her scales mostly covered her, though technically they were just a part of her skin. Which made her naked again in her book, though she could understand why a lot of people would disagree. She did feel less exposed when she was wearing them after all.

The blue-haired man looked at her intently, worry etched on his face. Now that was interesting. He didn't have anything to be worried about as far as she knew. But it did raise questions about what he was doing down here in the first place.

And what he was looking for.

Curiosity got the better of her, and Amber began the transformation into her half shifted form. Her face and hair returned to normal. Her body shrunk dramatically, and the grey-green scales retracted until they were covering all of her skin up past her breasts. At least she was decent.

Blue-hair's eyes widened as he took her in.

"You can half-shift?" he asked.

Odd question. She'd have many more if she were him.

"Obviously."

"But not your tail?"

She scowled at him. But really, how was he to know her tail had been removed. She'd long since given up telling any of Ben Vair's staff when she lost it. They just didn't care.

"My tail and I had an unfortunate separation," she replied.

His gaze travelled the length of her body, making her particularly self-conscious. No non-beithir had ever seen her like this, and it was an unusual situation to find herself in.

"Unfortunate how?"

"Tamsin," she replied stiffly, holding her head up high. She wasn't going to let anyone see how much she hated being without a tail.

"The annoying wolf shifter girl?" he asked.

"Yes. Are you sure you're a teacher?"

He certainly wasn't acting like it, and she wasn't sure she liked it.

"Yes, yes, whatever."

Amber frowned at him.

"What are you looking for?" she asked as he glanced around the lab again.

"I can't tell you that." His response was instant, and pretty definite. Then again...

"What if I agreed not to tell anyone you were down here. Or that you were looking for something. Or that you're clearly not a teacher?" She squared of against him, and his features took on a concerned look. Good. She was getting to him then.

Blue-hair smiled slightly. "You swear it?

"On the stub of my tail."

"I'm looking for a ruby infused with baobhan sìth saliva." He sighed, and pushed a hand over his face, leaving his blue hair in slight disarray. She almost reached out and smoothed it down. Almost.

"And you think you'll find it in here?" She could almost laugh. He was in completely the wrong part of the underground rooms to find anything like that.

"At least you think it exists," he pointed out.

"Of course it exists. Otherwise you wouldn't be looking for it. But why in the clouds would you want one of those?" She didn't even know what one did.

Probably something icky if there was a incubus involved. Not that incubi themselves were icky creatures. Nor was sex with one, but there were a lot of ill uses to their magic according to rumour, and she dreaded to think what some of those could be.

"I wish I knew." He looked away and shuffled his feet, so she dropped it. Despite really wanting to know, she didn't want to make him uncomfortable. She had a feeling he knew a lot of interesting things. And she wanted to learn them all if she could. And more.

After Ben Vair, she'd been planning on journeying all over the world, and discovering creatures like her but by other names. She was sure there were some after all.

"You're looking in the wrong place."

"Huh?"

"You're not going to find a ruby in what is effectively a biology lab."

"How do you even know what biology is," he muttered, quite possibly not meaning for her to hear.

Amber hissed, the sound coming across more menacing due to her half-shifted form. "I'm a mythical being, not an idiot. Try and remember that."

He gulped, and nodded. "Sorry, lead on, please."

She relaxed a little. It wasn't his fault he was so ill informed. But if she ever met the people who'd raised him...well they were going to get a piece of her mind.

4

When he'd set off to find the items on his grandfather's list, the last thing he'd expected was to be following a partially shifted beithir around dingy corridors under a school. And yet...here he was. Mostly being very glad she was eighteen, as his gaze kept drifting back to the greenish grey shine of her scales as the light passed over them. It didn't take a genius to work out they were all she was wearing. Even if she hadn't changed form in front of him. She'd given a longing glance towards her folded clothes, then shaken her head before they set off. He didn't blame her. The scaly skin encasing her body acted as another layer of protection. While he knew she wouldn't need it from him, she didn't.

"Are you sure you know where we're going?" he asked.

"Yes."

"How?" It was a little convenient if anyone asked him. He was looking for something, and she just so happened to know where it was? And just so happened to be here at the same time he was? He wasn't a fan of coincidences, and this stunk of one.

Briefly, he wondered if his grandfather had sent her as a way of testing him. But he doubted it. While his grandfather was fine with using other supernatural creatures, other than the *aos sìth*, he held very little respect for them. Particularly shifters. Izban's grandfather was one of the people that believed the animal side of the brain started to take over. And the more a shifter changed form, the more animal they became. Izban had long since dismissed it as the wrong opinion.

"They gave me a key to use the lab any time I lose my tail. Which happens a lot. I'd be a bad student if I didn't explore at least a little bit."

"Is it not being a bad student to go places when you shouldn't?" he threw back at her, and she chuckled throatily, a small hiss coming out at the end of it. Her voice box wasn't totally human at this point then. Interesting, if completely useless to know.

He wondered if she was poisonous in human form too, though he wasn't in any hurry to figure that one out.

"Isn't it a bad teacher to come to a school just so you can find something you want?"

"Not to a school like this. I'm not sure you can even call it that. A holding place for teenagers, more like."

"It's not that bad," she said defensively, but then went quiet. "Okay, you're right. I think the only knowledge that will actually help me in real life has come from books. Being taught together with mages and other more magical species isn't a good way to improve your beithir skills."

She sighed, then quickly changed the topic. "So what are you when you don't pretend to be a teacher?"

"Don't laugh," he warned her, before half-whispering, "A meteorologist."

She snorted. "You're joking, right?"

"I told you not to laugh," he complained, but there was a trace of humour in his voice. He got that reaction a lot. But his affinity with the weather had made his career choice an easy one. He had always liked being out and about, learning about weather phenomenon and exploring other countries in the process. Last year, he'd been on a research trip to the Arctic. That's where he learned that he was different from other humans, not just because of his magic. He didn't have any problem with staying in such a cold place. In fact, he felt better there than he ever had in the temperate climates he'd grown up in. He spent as much time as possible outside the research station, much to the worry of his supervisor. Walking through snow made him feel more alive than ever before. It was heartbreaking when he had to leave and return to the UK. Everything felt too warm here, despite other people complaining about the cold.

This winter, he was going to return to the Arctic. Doing these jobs for his grandfather would ensure that he could afford it. And he'd met her in the process. He really shouldn't complain.

"Is it much further?" he asked, trying to stop her laughing. Come on, him being a meteorologist wasn't that strange. Her walking around with only half a tail was much more unusual. But he was wise enough not to say that. Her teeth had looked incredibly dangerous. Being bitten by a beithir was not on his agenda.

"Just around the corner."

He followed the scaled girl to the end of the corridor where she turned sharp left. There were five doors and she chose the second. He'd never have found this place. What luck it had been to run into her.

She went into the room first, switching on the lights. Magical ones, of course, there was no electricity in this old part of the building.

He sighed as he took in the chaos in front of him. It looked like someone had discarded all of his artefacts and magical equipment and thrown it carelessly into this room. There were hundreds of boxes of all sizes, some of them open and spilling their contents, some locked with heavy chains. The shelves lining the walls were not much tidier; in fact, Izban doubted that even the owner of this room would ever find anything important in here.

This was like finding a needle in a haystack. Except that a haystack was a lot safer than a room full of magical items that might fight back.

"Are you sure the ruby is in here?" he asked his guide, resigned to spending several days in there, combing through all the boxes.

"Of course. Can't you smell it?"

He frowned at her. "Smell it? Since when do gemstones smell?"

She chuckled. "Not the ruby, silly. The incubus."

"How do you know what an incubus scent is like? Have you met many of them?"

She seemed far too innocent for that. She may even still be a virgin, growing up in a place so far away from any decent civilisation. Poor girl, she was not going to be prepared for the real world when she left Ben Vair.

"Of course. My godfather is one."

"Your..." he spluttered. "And you're okay with that?"

She laughed lightly. "Don't be so prejudiced. They are people like you and me, and most can control their urges. Or live them out in a way that doesn't hurt anybody."

"But... I'm not sure I'd want an incubus around my children."

She laughed again. "Wait until you meet him. Then you might think differently."

What did she mean by that? What were the chances of him meeting her godfather? She was just helping him find that ruby, right? And then expected him to leave and never meet again?

Or was she looking for more?

She moved around the room, sniffing the air while carefully stepping over boxes. "It's not far, I've smelled it before."

"Do I even want to know?" he asked, grimacing slightly. Incubi were an interesting species for him to wrap his head around. He'd only ever heard tales of what they could achieve, but even they terrified him. The loss of control, and the influence they could have...just no.

"They go for a lot of money, and Uncle Morris was a little short, so he made one."

"Morris?" That wasn't a name he'd imagine an incubus having.

"Yes, Uncle Morris. He met my Dad when they competed against each other in some sort of supernatural Olympics for teenagers."

"What a mouthful," Izban muttered.

"Quite. Now shhh please while I try and find the ruby."

He watched as she sniffed the air, her stub of a tail waggling slightly as she did. She was probably trying to use it for balance as a reflex. The image tugged on something inside him. She couldn't be comfortable tail-less. It was likely what losing a hand or foot would feel like to him.

"How often do they take your tail?" he asked

despite himself, drawing a dirty look from the beithir.

She chose to ignore him and wandered further into the cluttered room, heading towards a large standing cupboard with a large amount of surety.

Cocking her head to the side, she twisted the handle and threw the doors open, revealing shelves laden with glittering jewels of all colours, shapes and sizes.

It was a pirates dream. Shame he wasn't one.

"They keep these beneath a school?"

"Where else would they keep them? No one really knows they're here." She searched through the cupboard, picking up the odd gem and examining it, before replacing it with a dissatisfied sigh.

"You do."

"Because I can smell them," she pointed out, this time choosing a small oval stone and lifting it to her nose.

"And the others can't?"

"Likely not. A beithir's sense of smell is one of the best in the world. Plus, they'd have to know what they were smelling, and as far as I know, there's no incubi or succubi here to recognise it."

"I'm sure someone else probably could." Other

people knew how the demon spawned races smelled, surely?

"Maybe, but they'd still need to be down here in the first place, and I certainly haven't seen any crowds."

"Well no..." he trailed off, already hating how wrong she was proving him. She was certainly a bright woman. As well as powerful, a deadly combination if ever he knew one.

And that was before anyone got to the poisonous teeth. They'd make all the difference in a fight.

"There you go then, perfect place to hide priceless artefacts." She replaced the small red stone, and picked up a bigger one, set into a gold chain with filigree edges. He wrinkled his nose at the garishness of the setting.

"Is that it?"

She nodded. "Yes, definitely it."

"Does it have to come set like that?"

A chuckle ending in a slight hiss drew his attention to her face. She was smiling, clearly at ease with him now. "Of course not, it's the ruby you want, not the necklace, but do you really have time to pry it out and make it different?" He shook his head. "Thought not."

"Thank you, Amber," he said, pocketing the stone, his hand brushing over his grandfather's list.

"You're welcome. It's not like it was doing anything sat in a cupboard down here. What do you need it for anyway?"

"I wish I knew," he replied. He sighed, pushing his hand over his face and messing up his hair. It was a good thing he wasn't overly conscious of his appearance, unless he counted wanting blue hair and a multitude of piercings, otherwise the gesture would have been far more frustrating.

"You've broken into a school and pretended to be a teacher for something you don't even know why you want?" Her voice lifted at the end, conveying her confusion. He couldn't blame her, he'd been confused ever since his grandfather had first given him the list.

"It's important."

"I'd hope so. I wouldn't like to think what the Headmistress would do to you if she found out. She likes to spit fire on a good day."

"That wouldn't be a problem," he responded, thinking of his own powers. Fire was unlikely to hurt him. And even if it did, he knew enough healing spells to be alright.

"If you say so, still wouldn't risk it for something I'm clueless about."

"I have a list," he admitted, annoyed with himself for caving to her so easily. But her curiosity was contagious, and he found himself wondering about the list for what was probably the first time. He should have asked his grandfather about it. That was his right as heir. And yet, he'd just been a good grandchild and done what he was told. Like he always had. And probably always would. Tradition went a long way for mages.

He studied Amber from the corner of his eye. She didn't look quite as young and innocent in this light as she had during their lesson on storms. Here, she looked like the dangerous creature she was. Maybe it was just because he'd seen her in her animal form. But he doubted it.

"Why were *you* down here?" he finally thought to ask.

"Regrowing my tail." She shrugged and closed the doors of the cupboard. She sauntered away from him, heading back towards the door they'd entered, so he had no chance to follow.

"That works?" He was surprised. Surely it wasn't as straightforward as that.

"No. I forgo sleep, and come hang out in the

creepiest part of the school, just for fun," she snapped. "Sorry, I'm just grumpy. It's not exactly fun losing a tail." Her tone was softer, and her apology seemed genuine.

"No, I'm sorry, that was insensitive of me." She nodded, not arguing back, and while he hated that, he knew she was in the right. "Is this really the creepiest part of the school?" He was proud of himself for deflecting with a change of subject, but regretted it when a slightly wicked smile crossed her lips.

"Probably not, no."

"What is?" he asked eagerly.

"Want me to show you?" she teased.

"Yes."

"Then follow this way."

5

"You know this building wasn't always used as a school?" she asked as they walked deeper into the catacombs. She'd explored them when she first came to the college. She may have used regrowing her tail as an excuse to justify her exploration to Izban, but in truth she was simply curious. Living in a place that she hadn't completely searched for anything interesting was no fun. So she'd spent dozens of nights walking through the endless tunnels beneath the school, enjoying the atmosphere of mystery and the forbidden. Strangely enough, there were few warded doors; the teachers probably thought that nobody would be interested in wandering so far into the maze of corridors. Luckily, Amber had an excellent sense of direction and only got lost a few times. And while her magic wasn't strong at all, she was able to summon a light bright enough to find her way. That wasn't to say that she hadn't occasionally stumbled on the uneven floor. Once she even broke through a decayed wooden trapdoor into a hidden chamber beneath. And that was exactly where she was leading Izban now.

"What was it before?" he asked as he followed her closely behind. She could almost feel his breath on her neck.

"It was used by the Shifter Government at some point, but before that, it was a prison. Do you believe in ghosts?"

He chuckled. "Not really, although some of your teachers might pass as one."

"Then let me change your mind."

They'd reached a small door, not much wider than Amber. It was going to be a slight squeeze for Izban. She still didn't know why anyone would build such a tiny door. It didn't make sense - but then, not a lot in this place made sense.

"Try not to offend her," she whispered and opened the door, revealing a dusty chamber that was likely host to a few hundred spiders. In the middle of the room was a large square hole in the floor; the place where the trapdoor had been before Amber had broken it.

"Bea? Are you there? I brought a visitor!" she called, peering down into the darkness beneath them. She'd only been in there once before and wasn't planning on repeating that experience. Bea didn't like people seeing her down there either. She preferred to come upstairs to welcome her one and only visitor - Amber.

Izban shrieked as Bea shimmered into being and Amber had a hard time stifling her snicker. He was pretending to be so strong and brave, but confront him with the ghost of a 17th century woman and he freaked out.

"What is she?" he shouted and the woman tsked.

"Don't you know it's impolite not to address the ghost in question?" Bea asked, adjusting her bonnet. She was in her fifties, an old age back in the times she lived in.

"S...Sorry," Izban stammered. "What are you?"

Bea chuckled and turned to Amber, who was watching the exchange with a wide smile on her lips. "Is he always this slow?"

"I wouldn't know, I only met him today."

"Well, he doesn't seem very bright. You may want to think about it before you start a relationship with him. I know how overwhelming young love can be."

Amber blushed and turned to hide her reddening cheeks. "You're daft, Bea. Now tell him what he wants to know."

The old ghost tsked again, then sat down in the air, crossing her legs until it looked like she was meditating.

"I'm dead, dear boy, and I've been a ghost for about three hundred years now. They let me starve in here, thinking I was a witch. Well, I wasn't, but my cellmate was. With her last breath, she wished that I would live - and she got her wish, even though it was not as she intended." She paused, seemingly lost in thought, until her eyes cleared and she began to stare at Izban.

"Is blue hair the fashion nowadays? I don't get out much, I don't like leaving my body behind."

Izban looked like he was tempted to look down into the chamber beyond the trapdoor, but Amber shook her head. The skeletons in there were not a pretty sight, nibbled on by generations of rats.

"I like it," he said defensively and the old woman chuckled.

"Oh, me too. I would get my hair dyed, if I could, but alas, it's destined to stay white, just like the rest of me. But Amber, darling, you've not come down here in a while. Tell me the latest gossip, will you, dear?"

"There's not much to tell you, Bea," she said, studying her clawed fingertips intensely.

"Really? Then how come you're stood here in your scales and not one of those gods awful baggy shirts you normally do?"

Amber shuffled from side to side, not sure what about this was making her so uncomfortable. It wasn't like Izban hadn't seen her in her normal clothes, it was what she wore to school every day. But something about it being brought up made her feel odd.

"I do that for my tail," she pointed out.

"Which you seem to have lost again." Bea didn't seem particularly concerned by that, nor surprised in the slightly.

Amber hissed.

"Don't hiss at me, young lady, it's not my fault you haven't given them a little nip and taught them not to mess with you," Bea scolded.

"You know I can't do that," she protested.

"Why not?" Both women's heads turned to the side in shock. Amber had almost forgotten Izban was in the room with them, and Bea seemed to have done the same.

"It could kill them," Amber admitted softly. "I may not want them ripping off my tail, but I also don't want them dead. It's terribly bad luck."

Izban chuckled softly.

"Ripping off your tail would be their bad luck if you bit them."

Bea's tinkling laugh filled the room. "I change my mind. Keep this one, Amber."

"He's not mine to keep," she muttered, her cheek flushing as she spoke. It wasn't even appropriate for Bea to suggest that. Not when he was her teacher. Except...no, he wasn't her teacher, he'd just been pretending. That opened a whole new level of complications.

"And I still don't see why you don't wear nicer clothes, Amber. Let everyone see the real you." Bea gave her a stern look. She did this almost every time Amber came to visit. She really seemed to hate the idea of Amber not reaching her full potential. At least it made her miss her own family less. With someone else watching out for her, there was definitely a comfort in that.

"The human's would likely have a fit if they saw I have a tail." Amber shrugged.

"Spell it?"

"That's not possible," Amber protested instantly.

"Seriously?" Bea raised an eyebrow, then turned to look at Izban rather than Amber. "Is it possible?"

"I've never tried, but I shouldn't think so. It'd just need a hiding spell placed on it," he replied, a thoughtful look on his face.

"That's beside the point," Amber interrupted. "I don't have any other clothes anyway, so it's not something I need to worry about."

"You don't have any clothes right now," Bea teased.

"I can summon them for you if you want, though?" Izban asked tentatively. Despite herself, Amber appreciated the offer. It seemed genuine too, as if he actually wanted to help her.

"My scales are fine, thank you."

The three of them lapsed into silence for a few moments. It was unusual for Bea to be quiet for so long, and Amber worried about that. She didn't want things to become awkward between her and her only friend at school.

"So tell me about you," Bea prompted Izban after a few moments. "Why are you here?"

Amber perked up at that. She was eager to find out what he'd been doing. And why he wanted such weird items.

"Erm..."

"You can tell us," Bea added. "Amber and I are very trustworthy."

Izban frowned, as if he was considering hard for just a few moments. "I have a list."

"Of..."

"Items."

"Cryptic," Amber added in exasperation. What was the point in only half opening up? He may as well have just stayed silent.

"Sorry, I'm not used to being able to say much about my abilities. I spend a lot of time around humans, you know what they're like."

Amber nodded. But Bea shook her head.

"Actually, no. I don't. I was a human until a mage spelled me, but I was clueless about the supernatural world until then. I'm not sure how humans would act. Especially humans now." She pouted, a highly amusing expression on a ghost. It'd probably be a lot more effective if she wasn't translucent.

"Sorry," Izban offered. "They're not very accepting of anything or anyone that's different. They're definitely not ready to know about our world."

"Good to know," Amber said, nodding her head.

"You didn't already?"

"No. I'm a beithir, remember? We basically live with our swarm in the mountains unless we're at school. Other than that, we fly in the storm clouds. We don't really interact with humans very much." She shrugged. It was probably something she should rectify. Especially if she didn't want to spend the rest of her life in the same place she was born.

"I didn't realise beithirs were so antisocial," he admitted.

"Explains a lot, right?" Bea teased. "Now, your list, young man."

"Yes." He rustled through his pocket and pulled out a worn piece of paper with words scribbled all over it. Amber's curiosity was piqued, and she leaned over to look down the list. Only getting annoyed with herself when she couldn't work what any of them meant. Except for *sgiathan sìthe*, but she had no idea what anyone would use a fairy's wings for. Other than fairies, naturally. She understood their use for their wings.

"Hand it over," Bea said, holding out a hand and making a grabbing motion.

Reluctantly, and with a clear expression of confusion on his face, Izban handed it over. Bea's spectral fingers closed around it, seeming surprisingly solid as she held the paper.

"Hmm." Her white brow furrowed, and a slither of anxiety wormed its way into Amber. Whatever it was, it didn't sound good.

"What is it?" Izban asked.

Amber was a little taken aback. Why didn't he know what was on the list? If she were him she'd have studied it time and time again, until she knew it by heart and could recite it aloud.

"Do you know what's on this?" Bea asked, her words coming out slowly as if she was still thinking about them.

"Yes, I memorised the list."

"Do you know what they are?" The same tone coloured her voice, though Amber didn't know if it was wariness of Izban, or over what was on it.

"Most of them yes."

"Who gave it to you?" This question came quicker, as if Bea was coming to actual conclusions and not just clutching at straws.

"My grandfather."

"Do you know why he's looking for the ingredients to gain immortality?"

6

Izban didn't speak while following Amber back into the main part of the school. His mind was far too busy mulling over what Bea had said. Immortality. He was having trouble getting his head around it. He knew his grandfather was having delusions of grandeur occasionally, but actually wanting to be immortal? No, that couldn't be right.

A tiny little voice in his head was telling him that it was a good idea, that if his grandfather wasn't to die, Izban wouldn't have to become Elder Mage. But that wasn't the point. There was a reason magic only appeared in every second generation. Izban's parents were as normal as humans went, although of course they'd grown up knowing that magic existed.

His father was even on the Mage Council, representing the non-magical mages, as they called themselves. But the jump in generations was so that younger people would take over their grandparents' roles, bringing new ideas and knowledge into the mix.

So for his grandfather to break that tradition... it was wrong. As much as he liked and respected the Elder Mage, Izban was not going to be an accomplice to him endangering their society's structure. If one of them somehow managed to become immortal, others would want to follow. There'd be fights, jealousy, maybe even deaths. No, he wasn't going to have any part in that.

He crumpled the list in his fist. If his grandfather wanted to do this, he was going to have to do it without his oldest grandson.

"Wait," he suddenly said and Amber stopped, looking at him expectantly. He was grateful that she had left him to his thoughts. Not many girls he knew would have done that.

"This ruby must be pretty rare, right?"

She shrugged. "I've never heard of any like it, but I'm not an expert in incubus-infused gem stones."

She winked and he had to smile. It was good to have her here with him. Maybe they could stay in touch after he left the school. Maybe she could go along on one of his meteorology expeditions...

"So if this one was to mysteriously disappear..."

"Then he'd have a hard time finding another. I like the way you think." She grinned at him and something near his stomach contracted. Maybe a bit below his belly. Like, between his legs. Nobody had ever had that effect on him, at least not after so short a time. They'd met maybe twelve hours ago and already he was thinking how he would like to spend more time with her, a lot more time.

He cleared his throat, trying to distract himself from her alluring smile.

"Same goes for that book about those horses, it looked so old that I doubt there are many copies lying around."

He unfolded the crumpled piece of paper he was still holding in his fist. There were a few rips in it, but the list was still legible. He showed it to Amber and she pointed at the final item.

"A hair of an Arran giant - weren't they supposed to be bald?"

"I've never even heard of them," Izban admitted. "Arran like the island?"

"Yes, there are giants' graves there and they even found a few remains nearby. Of course the humans believed it was a hoax, but the bones were taken to a lab in Edinburgh where one of my distant relatives works."

"There are beithirs who work among humans?" Izban asked in surprise.

"It's a supernatural lab, but yes, not all of us are as reclusive as my family. It takes a lot of effort to blend in when you have a tail."

"So you're saying that there is no Arran Giant hair because they were bald? Then why is it on this list?"

Amber shrugged. "All I know is that they think they were bald, but they only found skeletons, so maybe they did have hair and we just don't know it? Anyway, I have no idea where that hair would be kept. Pretty sure it's not in this school."

"Well, that makes it easier for me not having to hide it. And this ruby... we could always destroy it. It's not like anyone would be able to find out what we did with it anyway."

She frowned. "How do you want to destroy it? It looks pretty solid to me."

He had an idea, but he wasn't sure if she'd be up for it. During their pretend lesson earlier that day, he'd felt her power, but it looked like she had no idea about it. He was going to have to be careful, he didn't want to make her feel inadequate or stupid. Because that was something she definitely wasn't. Untrained, yes. Stupid, not at all.

"I think lightning might destroy it," he said in as neutral a voice as possible. "With enough energy pressed into the ruby, it might shatter."

"And where are we going to get lightning from? Are you going to ask Thor to come down from Asgard?"

Thunder rolled over the school and they both jumped, bumping into each other. They stepped back, avoiding each other's eyes. Izban could still feel his skin tingle where she'd touched him. He was almost hoping for another bout of thunder to make her do the same thing.

They'd reached the main entrance hall. It was empty; everyone was in bed.

"I'm a meteorologist, did you forget? I knew it was going to storm tonight. Now we just need to find a way to conduct lightning into the stone."

"Is that something you can do?" she asked, still not aware of what he was getting at.

He took a deep breath. "No, but I believe you may be able to."

"No." She shook her head profusely, her hair whipping against her cheeks as she did. She could feel the power of the storm brewing above them, but she knew as well as anyone that she wouldn't be able to harness it.

She wasn't old enough.

She wasn't powerful enough.

She just wasn't enough.

"I think you can," Izban tried to assure her.

"I've never been able to control lightning, I don't know why you think I'll suddenly be able to do it now."

"Will power is a powerful thing," he pointed out, just annoying her rather than anything else. How would he know anyway. He wasn't a beithir. He just had mage powers. And while she didn't know how they worked exactly, she doubted they'd be the same. Especially because they seemed to be teachable, whereas beithir powers were just innate at birth. It was only once they'd manifested in the beithir's twenties that they were able to actually learn how to harness them properly.

And only ever from another beithir too. She'd always imagined it'd be her mother who taught her.

"I can't do it."

"Please, try. We haven't lost anything if you can't do it. And if you can, well we're further ahead than we were before."

She studied him intently. He seemed to be being earnest, but it was hard to tell. She really didn't know him that well. Or at least, not as well as she should to be making these kind of assumptions.

"Fine, I can try. But I'm not promising anything."

"Good. What do you need?"

"How should I know? It may have escaped your notice, but I've not done anything like this before," she bit out.

"Sorry, I forgot for a moment. You said you lived in the mountains, right?"

"Yes..." She drew out the word, wondering where he was going with this.

"We could go up the one behind the school?"

She nodded. That was a reasonable suggestion, and she was a little bit miffed she hadn't come up with it herself. It was kind of obvious now she was thinking about it.

"Okay."

"Do you know how to get there?" he asked after a moment's silence. She let out the laugh that was building within her.

"Of course I know. I haven't spent years at this school and not explored everywhere I can."

"When you weren't supposed to be, no doubt."

"Nope, none at all. There's the thing with being a giant poisonous reptile. Other than the odd bully, most people tend to leave you to your own business."

"Just how poisonous are you?" His brow furrowed as he studied her, and she smiled at him sweetly.

"You don't want to find out."

"Meaning you don't know." He smirked at her, and she had to admit being amused he'd worked it out so quickly.

"Not really, no, and I'm not in a hurry to find out. But fully mature beithir poison can kill most things. I'm not far off from that point, so I'd advise against getting in the way of my teeth."

He laughed, the sound deep and throaty,

travelling through Amber far more than she expected, or was comfortable with. These weren't reactions she was used to or expecting. And she wasn't completely sure how best to deal with them.

"I'll keep that in mind."

"Good." They stood in slightly awkward silence for a moment. Probably partly due to the fact Amber's mind had wandered off to situations where him being in the way of her teeth might not be so bad. Her human teeth anyway...

She shook her head, trying to rid herself of the images. Now wasn't the time.

"Shall we get going?" she asked him after clearing her throat.

Izban jumped slightly, as if being drawn out of his own thoughts too. "Yes, let's. How long will it take to get there?"

"It depends. How averse are you to flying?" An idea was forming in her head, and she was eager to try it out. She might not have ever had anyone on her back before, but it sounded like a great challenge to fly so they could stay there. She just hoped Izban was strong enough to hold on.

"I don't know a spell for that, sorry."

"I wasn't talking about a spell," she responded, a wicked grin twisting at her lips.

She performed a quick half shift, before ridding herself of the clothing she'd put back on after leaving Bea. Then, she performed one of the quickest full shifts of her life. Probably because it was happening so closely to her previous one. She didn't think she'd ever shifted twice in one day before. Not since she was a child anyway.

She stretched her neck from side to side, before lowering her head to lay next to Izban.

An uneasy look graced his face, but she didn't really blame him. Not many people would be comfortable if a giant reptile presented them with its neck.

"Are you sure, Amber?"

Oh, she liked how he said her name. And how he was actually checking that it was okay. In fact, she liked that a lot. It said something about him.

She nodded her large head up and down. He sighed, stepping towards her. Maybe his question was more to do with his own fears than wanting to make sure she was comfortable.

Well, no matter the reason, it was a good thing.

Carefully, and a little reluctantly, she felt Izban climb onto her neck, swinging his left leg over so he was straddling her. It felt odd to have someone sat there, but not as unpleasant or intrusive as she expected. He gripped onto the mane of scales that travelled down her back, and she chuckled inwardly. That was a use for them that she'd never thought of before. It'd help his grip though.

Amber gave him a few moments to get comfortable, before using the lower part of her body, including her tail stub, to propel herself off the ground and into the air.

Izban let out an involuntary scream, and she laughed to herself again. If she was feeling particularly mean, then she'd have done some aerobatic tricks while she was flying, but she didn't think he'd appreciate those. Plus, she'd feel more than a little guilty if she dropped him.

There'd be a lot of questions too. Questions she wasn't sure she really wanted to answer.

Her family would likely be horrified she'd let someone ride on her anyway. Never mind the fact there'd be a dead body to deal with.

Izban's screams of surprise soon turned into shouts of enjoyment as the wind rushed past them. If she'd been human, she'd have smiled. There certainly was something about the rush and anticipation of a storm. She was glad he could feel it too.

Non-magical people might wonder why

someone who was basically a snake without wings could fly. Well... magic. She didn't quite know how it worked, but she'd never crashed so that was all that counted. And it seemed like she could even carry a passenger without much trouble.

Izban was really enjoying himself. His thighs gripped her body tightly, but his arms were in the air, embracing the wind that was surrounding them. Sometimes she felt as if the elements wanted to play with her when she was flying. Especially during storms when the wind would push her from side to side, but never hurting her. It was a beautiful feeling that she got far too seldom. She wished she was back living in the highlands with her family, with no humans around who could spot her. Here at the college, she rarely went out to fly; they were too close to populous areas. And the winds here just weren't the same as the gales over the mountains.

Thunder rolled close by and Izban fell silent for a moment. Was he afraid? But he cheered again and she knew he was fine. Lightning flashed in the distance and she was tempted to fly closer, but that wouldn't be safe. Everybody knew lightning was dangerous, even if her heart didn't believe it.

The top of the mountain came closer and she began her decent, slithering downwards, trying to be gentle. When she was alone, she did some daring manoeuvres, but not with Izban on her back. Maybe for their next flight.

She sighed when she landed on the wet grass that covered the mountain top. She already missed the feeling of weightlessness, but she had a job to do. She shifted into her human, but scaled, form as soon as Izban had slid off her back.

It was cold and wet, but the drizzling rain pearled off her scales. She was made for this weather. The mage next to her, not so much. His blue hair was wet on his scalp, missing its usual spring and volume. His clothes were soaked, but with a swish of his hands, he had them dry again. But it wouldn't last long; the rain seemed to increase. So did the thunder and lightning. The centre of the storm was about to pass over them.

"Do you have the ruby?" she asked and he pulled it out of his pocket. It was a beautiful stone, really, perfectly polished and smooth. "Do you really want to destroy it?"

He stroked the ruby with a finger. "My precioussssss," he growled and she laughed. A geeky mage? Why yes, please.

"And yes, let's destroy it," he said when they'd both stop laughing, now serious again. "If we lay it on this rock here and stand back, do you think you can direct a bolt of lightning onto it?"

She huffed. "That sounds a little too much like something I'd have to have practiced several times to get it right. I don't want you to be the one who gets hit by lightning, nor me. No, it's probably best if we leave the mountain and fly close by. My magic is strongest when I'm shifted anyway."

"You can do magic when you're a snake... ehm... beithir?" he asked in bewilderment.

"Yes, you should try it," she quipped and took the ruby from his hand, studying it closely. The stone Izban had mentioned was a large boulder right next to them with a smooth top that seemed an ideal place to lay the gemstone. If the rain didn't get any heavier, she'd be able to spot the boulder from afar without being too close to the lightning she was supposed to conjure. Not that she knew how to do that. But it was time to find out if she could learn.

"Let's do this. I'll shift and you get back on. I may have to put you down somewhere though if I need to climb higher. It's not safe in the clouds for someone who isn't a natural lightning rod."

He nodded and without waiting for him to say anything further, she shifted. She hadn't changed shapes this often in one day for a long time. Maybe she should do it more often; it was freeing to leave one shape behind and take on another.

Izban climbed onto her back, already knowing how best to keep a good hold on her. She had to admit, they were quite the team. She pushed herself into the air, squealing inside as they left the mucky ground behind. That was one disadvantage of beithirs, they didn't have any vocal chords, so she couldn't even laugh or cheer while she was flying. But in her head, she laughed wildly at the exhilarating feeling of flying through the storm.

When she was at a safe distance from the mountain top, she stopped in mid-air, turning around until she could see the stone their ruby was lying on. Rain was pouring down and dripping over her eyes, but she was made to be waterproof, so it didn't bother her too much.

Now came the tricky part. She could feel the electricity sizzling in the clouds above her, but how was she going to get it to form into lightning and then hit the exact spot she wanted it to?

She tried reaching out with all her senses, like they had taught her at school. She knew there was magic all around her, she just didn't know how to access it. Somehow, she'd always known that her magic wasn't about creating things - that's why she'd never be able to create a storm - but about manipulating existing elements to do her bidding. Like these clouds bristling with energy, just waiting to be released. They were so close, all she had to do was give them a slight push and...

Lightning tore through the air, crashing into the ground faster than she could see. But it was the wrong bit of ground. Another hilltop, to be precise, and not the one the ruby was on.

Mmhm. She knew that lightning couldn't hurt her - she'd learned that as a child - so theoretically she could get closer... but not with Izban on her back. It was going to be more boring without him, but it couldn't be helped.

She flew to the ground, not where they'd started, but the closest and safest bit she could find. Not high enough to be a target for lightning to strike, not low enough to take forever to get to.

He slid off her back. "Good luck," he whispered, gently stroking her scales.

She savoured the feeling for a moment, then flew off, high into the nearest cloud.

The storm was picking up, and beginning to get dangerous. For other people at least. She was glad she'd set Izban down. There was a chance he'd be able to perform some kind of protection spell, but she didn't really want to risk it. Not if she wanted to try and get him to watch a film with her after this. Or maybe the latest TV show with dragons and wars. It'd be better if there were beithirs in it, but apparently too many people had forgotten they'd even existed in mythology for anyone to put them in anything.

Her scales tingled, and she knew another bolt of lightning was about to strike close to her. Maybe she could harness this one. It crackled around her, and she was sure there were little bolts of electricity dancing over her scales and lighting her up. It must look beautiful from where Izban was standing. She'd once seen her cousin do this, and she'd not been able to do anything but stare.

Feeling the power, she tried to drag it into her. This was how it was supposed to work. Yet, it didn't work.

She tried again, imagining the process in as much detail as she could, and slowly, it began to work. A ball of electricity began to build inside her, feeding off the lightning surrounding her. By now, she was likely lighting up the sky. Humans would just put it down to a weird natural phenomenon, much like they did with the Northern Lights. They were woefully blind to the supernatural world around them.

She dipped lower in the sky, dragging the lightning with her and trying her best not to let it go. She'd only have one shot at this. If she got it wrong, then she wasn't too sure she'd be able to draw enough lightning into her again. Or if the storm had enough to give. Scotland was notoriously fickle in its weather patterns. Amber couldn't rely on it.

She set her sights on the rock with the ruby on it, hoping she hadn't picked out the wrong one. She focused all her thoughts on sending the lightning to that particularly spot, the concentration almost enough to cause a headache. Impressive given she didn't think she had the capacity for one in this form.

Within seconds, the lightning began to travel through her. The surge of power was like nothing she'd ever felt before. It was euphoric. Beyond anything she could possibly imagine. And more. It was something to admire and be terrified of. And she loved it. She wanted more. Always more. Always power.

The lightning crashed down to earth, at precisely the point she wanted to hit, and she smiled inwardly, pleased with herself for how well her attempt at actual magic had worked.

"WELL DONE LITTLE BEITHIR. YOU THWARTED MY PLAN," a Voice boomed through her head, causing a ripple of her terror throughout her body. That'd never happened before. Maybe it was one of the thunder gods? But no, it couldn't be. It'd long since been accepted in the supernatural community that the gods didn't exist. At least, not anymore.

The last of the electricity left her body and crashed into the earth. Amber's eyes began to flicker closed, and no matter what she tried, she couldn't seem to manage to stay alert.

Which was concerning given how far above the earth she was. At least she probably wouldn't die in this form. She had a lot more bounce to her than when she was a flesh and blood human.

That thought wasn't particularly helping.

Her eyes closed again, and this time, it took her even longer than before to open them.

A sudden jerk woke her up a little more, especially when she realised she'd dropped about thirty feet through the air. That was never good.

"COME TO ME," the Voice boomed.

It must be her imagination.

It had to be.

Her eyes flickered closed again.

She jerked back.

The blackness came quicker this time.

More height lost.

At least the earth was closer this time.

8

Izban watched in elation as Amber managed to direct electricity towards where they'd left the ruby. If only he could check it'd been destroyed. Anything to stop his grandfather from gaining power and upsetting the balance of the mage society. But without Amber, he couldn't get back up there.

He smiled to himself as he thought about their flight. It'd been exhilarating in a way he'd never expected, nor truly experienced before. Amber was a truly remarkable woman, and her skills in the air had allowed him to completely let go during their flight. He wasn't sure where his trust in her had come from, but he liked it, it meant he could truly enjoy her company.

And he couldn't wait to enjoy it more. Maybe he'd even take up a teaching post at Ben Vair. It wasn't like he could return home now. His grandfather would probably have him as a traitor.

He shook the thoughts away, and looked back up into the sky just as the last of the electricity was leaving Amber's body. It was a truly magnificent sight, and he was honoured to have had the opportunity to watch.

She hovered there for a moment, her majestic body swishing back and forth in the wind, her tail streaming out behind her. The surge of magic must have caused it to regrow. That was something at least. He smiled. She'd like having it back. He'd been able to tell how much it pained her to not have it.

He could understand. Missing a body part couldn't be a pleasant sensation, no matter which body part that was.

Suddenly, she dropped several feet through the air, and Izban's heart rose to his throat, thudding away there as concern began to build. She hadn't shown any signs of a loss of control while the two of them had been flying. Yet here she clearly had.

She dropped again, and he lurched forward, holding out his hands and trying to reach out to her. Which was ridiculous, he knew that. But something much bigger than either of them was propelling him further.

When she dropped again, the panic began to get way too much. Something was very, very, wrong up there.

This time, she fell. And he felt the rumble through the mountain floor as she hit the ground. Panic filled him and he really hoped her beithir form was strong enough to take the hit.

Even so, he found himself moving towards where she'd probably ended up, calling his *aos sìth* with a twist of his ring as he did. The creature would be incredibly pissed that he was being summoned again, but right now, Izban didn't care. Even if the creature turned on him after this it'd be worth it. Though it wouldn't. He'd just appease it with plenty of offerings.

"Lorg beithir," he demanded of the *aos sìth*. It looked at him, unimpressed, and cocked it's head to the side. Maybe it didn't recognise the reptile as an object. Which was fair. It wasn't. *"Lorg Amber,"* he tried instead. The *aos sìth* thought for a moment, and then flew off into the night.

Hurriedly, Izban followed behind, not at all surprised that it wasn't long before the creature came to a halt. It flew round and round in a circle, chittering loudly.

The ground was dented, like something large had hit it. Something like a giant snake-dragon. "Amber," Izban whispered into the night. Where was she? There was next to no chance she'd been conscious after a fall like that. So she should be here. "Where is she?" he asked his *aos sìth*, who just pointed at the crater and spun around in a circle then.

Well, that was no help. None at all.

"Amber?" Izban called out into the night. But with the storm already calming, and the place being abandoned, it wasn't surprising no one answered.

Instead, an almost deathly silence filled the clearing. This wasn't good. And only one thought filled his head. He had to find her. If it was the last thing he did, he had to. He owed her that at the very least for helping him with a problem he didn't know existed.

Without thinking about it, he unsheathed the *sgain-dubh* he kept in his waistband. Not the traditional place to keep the dagger, he knew, but a traditional kilt would have been highly impractical given the situation. Not to mention, the knife may have aroused suspicion he didn't need.

He sliced the blade down his palm, and watched as the blood welled up there. His *aos sìth* chattered loudly in alarm, realising what it was he was doing, and the potential repercussions of it. Izban didn't let it stop him.

"*Gheibh mi greim ort, Amber A' Bheithir,*" he swore. "I'll find you, Amber. I promise."

This is where Through the Storms *ends, but it's only the beginning of Amber and Izban's journey.*

Stay in their world for a while longer by reading From the Deeps, *#1 in the Seven Wardens Series, where you'll also meet Izban again.*

Both he and Amber play a major role later on in the series, starting with the second book, Into the Mists.

ABOUT LAURA GREENWOOD

Laura is a USA Today Bestselling Author of paranormal, fantasy, and urban fantasy romance (though she can occasionally be found writing contemporary romance). When she's not writing, she drinks a lot of tea, tries to resist French macarons, and works towards a diploma in Egyptology. She lives in the UK, where most of her books are set.

Follow the Author

- Website: www.authorlauragreenwood.co.uk
- Mailing List: www.authorlauragreenwood.co.uk/p/mailing-list-sign-up.html
- Facebook Group: http://facebook.com/groups/theparanormalcouncil
- Facebook Page: http://facebook.com/authorlauragreenwood

- Bookbub: www.bookbub.com/authors/
  laura-greenwood

facebook.com/authorlauragreenwood
twitter.com/lauramg_tdir
instagram.com/authorlauragreenwood
bookbub.com/authors/laura-greenwood
amazon.com/author/lauragreenwood

ABOUT SKYE MACKINNON

Skye MacKinnon is a USA Today & International Bestselling Author whose books are filled with strong heroines who don't have to choose.

She embraces her Scottishness with fantastical Scottish settings and a dash of mythology, no matter if she's writing about Celtic gods, cat shifters, or the streets of Edinburgh.

When she's not typing away at her favourite cafe, Skye loves dried mango, as much exotic tea as she can squeeze into her cupboards, and being covered in pet hair by her demon cat Sootie.

Subscribe to her newsletter:
skyemackinnon.com/newsletter

Join her Facebook group:
facebook.com/groups/skyesbookharem

facebook.com/skyemackinnonauthor
twitter.com/skye_mackinnon
instagram.com/skyemackinnonauthor
bookbub.com/authors/skye-mackinnon
goodreads.com/SkyeMacKinnon
amazon.com/author/skye_mackinnon

www.ingramcontent.com/pod-product-compliance
Lightning Source LLC
Chambersburg PA
CBHW031748150726
47989CB00006B/2638